Monsieur Ibrahim
and the Flowers of the Koran

...lay i...
by another

PO Box 191
Tadworth
Surrey KT20 5YQ

email: info@acornbook.co.uk

www.acornbook.co.uk

ISBN 0-9544959-2-6

British Library Cataloguing in Publication Data.
A catalogue record for this book is available from the British Library.

Originally published as Monsieur Ibrahim et les Fleurs du Coran
Copyright © Editions Albin Michel S.A., 2001, 2002
Translated from the French by Marjolin de Jager
English language translation copyright © Other Press 2003
This edition copyright © acorn book company 2004
Printed and bound in Great Britain by Cromwell Press Ltd.

We would like to thank the Arts Council
of England for their assistance
in the publication of this title.

This book is supported by the French Ministry for
Foreign Affairs, as part of the Burgess programme
headed for the French Embassy in London by the
Institut Français du Royaume-Uni.

For Bruno Abraham-Kremer

Monsieur Ibrahim

and the Flowers of the Koran

Eric-Emmanuel Schmitt

When I was eleven years old I broke open my piggy bank and went to see the whores.

My piggy bank was made of glazed porcelain, the colour of vomit, with a slit that allowed you to put coins in but not to take them out. My father had chosen it, this one-way piggy bank, because it matched his outlook on life—money is made to be saved, not spent.

There were two hundred francs inside the pig's belly. Four months of work.

One morning, before I left for school, my father said:

'Moses, I don't understand... There's money missing... From now on, when you do the shopping I want you to write down everything you spend in the kitchen ledger.'

So it wasn't enough that I was being yelled at both in school and at home, that I had to clean, study, cook, do the shopping. It wasn't enough that I was living alone in a large, dark flat that was empty and loveless, that I was a slave rather than the son of a lawyer who did not have much business anymore and no wife. I now had to be treated like a thief as well! Since he already suspected me of stealing, I might as well just do it.

So there were two hundred francs inside the piggy bank. Two hundred francs—that's what a girl cost in the Rue de Paradis. It was the price of becoming a man.

The first few asked me for my identity card. In spite of my voice and my size—I was as big as a horse—they seemed to doubt that I was sixteen, although that is what I told them. They must have seen me walk by and grow up over these past years, hooked onto my shopping bags full of vegetables.

At the end of the street beneath an overhang stood a new one. She was plump and pretty as a picture. I showed her my money. She smiled.

'You're sixteen, are you?'

'Sure, since this morning.'

We went upstairs. I could barely believe it, she was twenty-two, she was old and she was all mine. She showed me how to wash and then how to make love.

Obviously, I already knew, but I let her tell me anyway so she'd be more at ease, and besides, I liked her voice, which was a little sullen, a little sad. The whole time, I was on the point of fainting. When we were done, she gently caressed my hair and said:

'You should come back and bring me a little present.'

That almost ruined my pleasure—I had forgotten the little present. There it was, I was a man, I'd had my baptism between the thighs of a woman, I could barely stand up because my legs were still shaking, and already the trouble had begun—I'd forgotten the famous little present.

I ran back to the flat, dashed into my room, looked around to see what I might give her that was most cherished, then ran back double speed to the Rue de Paradis. The girl was beneath the overhang again. I gave her my teddy bear.

It was around that time that I first got to know Monsieur Ibrahim.

Monsieur Ibrahim had always been old. In the memory of everyone in the Rue Bleue and the Rue du Faubourg-Poissonnière, it was agreed that, from eight o'clock in the morning until the middle of the night, they had always seen Monsieur Ibrahim in his shop squashed between his till and the cleaning products, one leg in the aisle and the other under the boxes of matches, a grey work shirt over a white dress shirt, ivory teeth beneath an austere moustache, and pistachio-coloured eyes—green and brown—lighter than his dark skin that bore the stains of wisdom.

For it was the general opinion that Monsieur Ibrahim was a sage. Probably because for at least forty years he had been the only Arab in a Jewish street. Probably because he smiled a lot and said little. Probably because he seemed untouched by the usual commotion of ordinary mortals, particularly Parisian mortals, never moving, like a branch grafted onto his stool, never clearing his stall for anyone to see, and vanishing between midnight and eight in the morning to nobody knew where.

So I did the shopping and made the meals everyday. I bought only canned food. If I went to buy it daily, it wasn't so it'd be fresh, no, but because my father would leave me money for just one day at a time, and besides, it was easier to cook that way!

When I began to steal from my father to punish him for having suspected me, I also started to steal from Monsieur Ibrahim. I was somewhat ashamed but, in order to struggle against my shame, I would think very hard when I paid him:

After all, he's only an Arab!

Every day I'd stare Monsieur Ibrahim straight in the eyes and that would give me courage.

After all, he's only an Arab.

'I'm not an Arab, Momo.

I'm from the Golden Crescent.'

I collected my groceries and went out into the street, stunned. Monsieur Ibrahim had heard me think! So, if he could hear me think, he knew I was ripping him off, too, perhaps?

The next day, I didn't take a single can but asked him: 'What is that, the Golden Crescent?'

I have to admit that all night long I had imagined Monsieur Ibrahim sitting on the point of a golden crescent flying through a starry sky.

'It's a region that goes from Anatolia to Persia, Momo.'

The following day, as I took out my wallet, I added:

'My name is not Momo but Moses.'

The day after that it was he who added:

'I know your name is Moses, that's exactly why I call you Momo. It's less grand.'

The following day as I was counting out my change, I asked:

'What does it matter to you? Moses is Jewish, not Arabic.'

'I'm not an Arab, Momo. I'm a Muslim.'

'So why do they say you're this street's only Arab

if you're not an Arab?'

'In the grocery business, Momo, Arab means 'open from eight in the morning until midnight and even on Sundays."

That's how the conversation went. One sentence a day. We had plenty of time. He, because he was old, and I, because I was young. And every other day I'd steal a can of food.

It would have taken us a year or two, I think, to have a one-hour conversation had we not met Brigitte Bardot.

Great excitement in the Rue Bleue. Traffic stopped. The street was closed off. They were shooting a film.

Anyone with a sex drive in the Rue Bleue, the Rue Papillon, and the Faubourg-Poissonnière was on alert. Women wanted to check and see if she was as fine as they said; men weren't thinking at all, whatever they might have to say was stuck in their fly. Brigitte Bardot is here! Wow, Brigitte Bardot in the flesh!

Me, I sat down at the window. I looked at her and

she made me think of the neighbours' cat on the fourth floor, a pretty little female cat who loves stretching in the sun on the balcony and seems to live, breathe, and wink only to arouse admiration. Looking more closely, I also discovered that she really resembled the whores of the Rue de Paradis without being aware that, actually, the whores of the Rue de Paradis disguised themselves as Brigitte Bardot to attract customers. Finally, to my utter amazement, I notice that Monsieur Ibrahim is standing in his doorway. It is the first time—at least since I've been alive—that he has left his stool.

Having watched the little Bardot creature flutter her wings in front of the cameras, I started thinking about the lovely blonde who owns my bear and I decided to go down to Monsieur Ibrahim's and take advantage of his inattention to pinch a few cans of food. Disaster! He's gone back to sit behind his till. His eyes are smiling above the soaps and clothes pegs as he watches Bardot. I've never seen him like this.

'Are you married, Monsieur Ibrahim?'

'Yes, of course I'm married.'

He isn't used to being asked any questions.

At that moment I could have sworn he wasn't as old as everyone thought.

'Monsieur Ibrahim! Imagine you are on a boat with your wife and Brigitte Bardot. Your boat is sinking. What do you do?'

'I bet my wife knows how to swim.'

I've never seen his eyes laugh like that. They're laughing uproariously, they're making a huge racket, those eyes.

Suddenly, action stations! Monsieur Ibrahim is standing at attention—Brigitte Bardot enters the shop!

'Good morning, Monsieur, would you have any water?'

'Of course, Miss.'

And then the unimaginable happens— Monsieur Ibrahim himself goes to get a bottle of water from a shelf and brings it to her.

'Thank you, Sir. How much do I owe you?'

'Forty francs, Miss.'

Brigitte gives a start. Me too. A bottle of water was worth about two francs at the time, not forty.

'I had no idea that water was so rare here.'

'It's not the water that is rare, Miss. It's real stars.'

He said it so charmingly, with such an irresistible smile, that Brigitte Bardot blushed a little, took out her forty francs, and went away.

I couldn't get over it.

'Really, Monsieur Ibrahim, you have some nerve.'

'Well now, my little Momo, I have to find some way to pay myself back for all the cans you've been pinching from me, don't I?'

That was the day we became friends.

It's true that from then on I could have gone elsewhere to steal my cans, but Monsieur Ibrahim made me swear that I wouldn't do that:

'Momo, if you must go on stealing, do it here, from me.'

Besides, during the days that followed Monsieur Ibrahim gave me lots of hints on how to extract money from my father without him realising it. Serving him bread, a day or two old, and putting it in the oven first; gradually adding more and more chicory to his coffee; reusing tea bags; mixing his usual Beaujolais with wine that cost three francs a bottle; and the crowning touch, the idea, the true idea, that proved that Monsieur Ibrahim was an expert in the art of screwing the world—replacing the country terrine with dog food.

Thanks to Monsieur Ibrahim's intercession, the adult world cracked, it no longer presented the same rock-solid wall I was always running into; a hand was held out to me through the crack.

I had saved two hundred francs again, and once more I could go and prove to myself that I was a man.

In the Rue de Paradis I went straight to the overhang where my bear's new owner stood. I brought her a shell someone had given me, a real shell that came from the sea, the real sea.

The girl smiled at me.

At that moment a man came running out of the alley fast as a hare, a whore chasing after him shouting:

'Thief! Thief! My bag!'

Without a moment's hesitation, I stuck out my leg. The thief stumbled a few yards and went sprawling. I jumped on him.

The thief looked at me, saw I was only a kid, smiled, ready to beat me up, but since the girl was charging down the street screaming louder and louder, he got up and ran off. Fortunately, the prostitute's shouting had given me muscles.

She came closer, teetering on her high heels. I handed her the bag that she clutched delightedly to her luscious bosom, so rich in bedroom sounds.

'Thank you sweetie. What can I do for you? You want me to give you a freebie?'

She was old. Thirty, at least. But Monsieur Ibrahim had always told me not to aggravate a woman.

'OK.'

And we went upstairs. My bear's owner looked very offended that her colleague had stolen me from her. When we walked by in front of her, she whispered in my ear:

'Come tomorrow. I'll give you a freebie, too.'

I didn't wait for the next day…

Monsieur Ibrahim and the whores made life with my father even more difficult. I began to do something terrible, something that baffled me—I was making comparisons. I was always cold when I was around my father. With Monsieur Ibrahim and the prostitutes, I felt warmer, lighter.

I would look at the great, lofty library he'd inherited, all those books that supposedly held the quintessence of the human mind, the A to Z of law, the subtlety of philosophy, and I would look at them in darkness—'Moses, close the shutters, the light will wreck the bindings'—and then I'd look at my father reading, alone in the circle of the floor lamp that stood over his pages like a yellow conscience. He was enclosed inside the walls of his scholarship, he paid me no more attention than he would a dog—besides, he hated dogs—he wasn't even tempted to throw me one bone of his knowledge. If I made a bit of noise:

'Oh, excuse me.'

'Moses, be quiet. I'm reading. I work, you see.'

Working, that was the important word, the absolute justification.

'I'm sorry, Dad.'

'Ah, it's a good thing your brother Popol wasn't like that.'

Popol was the other name for my worthlessness. My father was always throwing the memory of my older brother, Popol, in my face whenever I did something wrong. 'Popol really applied himself at school. Popol loved maths and he never made the bath dirty. Popol didn't pee next to the toilet. Popol liked reading books just as much as Dad.'

In the end, it wasn't so bad that my mother had left with Popol not too long after I was born, because fighting a memory was hard enough already, but having to exist side by side with living perfection such as Popol, that would have been too much for me.

'Dad, do you think Popol would have liked me?'

My father stared at me, or rather, in great alarm tried to decode me.

'What a question!'

That's the answer I got: What a question!

I had learned to look at people with my father's eyes. With mistrust and disdain. Talking with the Arab shopkeeper, even if he wasn't an Arab—since in the grocery business, 'Arab' means being open nights and Sundays—and doing favours for whores were things I put in a secret drawer of my mind, they weren't officially part of my life.

'Why don't you ever smile, Momo?' Monsieur Ibrahim asked me.

That was a real blow, that question, a punch in the gut, and I wasn't prepared.

'Smiling is something rich people do, Monsieur Ibrahim. I can't afford it.'

Just to wind me up he started to smile.

'You think I'm rich, then?'

'You've got bank notes in your till all the time. I don't know anyone who has so much money to look at all day long.'

'But these notes are for paying for the merchandise and then the rent as well. And by the end of the month I have very little left over, you know.'

And he smiled even more as if to mock me.

'Monsieur Ibrahim, when I tell you that smiling is something rich people do, I mean that it's for happy people.'

'Well now, that's where you are all wrong. It's smiling that makes you happy.'

'Yeah, sure.'

'Try it.'

'Sure, I said.'

'You're a polite boy, though, aren't you, Momo?'

'I have to be, or else I get smacked.'

'Polite is good. Friendly is better. Try smiling, you'll see.'

Fine. After all, when asked nicely by Monsieur Ibrahim, who handed me a can of *choucroute garnie* on the sly, it was worth trying.

The next day, I really behave like a sick person who caught something during the night—I'm smiling at everybody.

'No, Miss, I apologise, I didn't understand the maths exercise.'

Wham—a smile!

'I just couldn't do it.'

'Well then, Moses, I'll explain it to you again.'

That's a new one. No shouting, no warning. Nothing.

In the canteen…

'May I have a little more of the chestnut purée, please?'

Wham—a smile!

'Yes, with some cream cheese.'

And they give it to me.

In the gym I realise I've forgotten my trainers.

Wham—a smile!

'They weren't dry yet, sir.'

The teacher laughs and pats me on the shoulder.

It's intoxicating. Nothing resists me any more. Monsieur Ibrahim has given me the perfect weapon. I'm strafing the whole world with my smile. Nobody is treating me like a pain in the neck any longer.

On the way home from school, I rush to the Rue de Paradis. I approach the most beautiful of the whores, a tall black woman who has always refused me:

'Hey!'

Wham—a smile!

'Shall we go up?'

'Are you sixteen?'

'Of course I'm sixteen. I have been for ages!'

Wham—a smile!

We go upstairs.

And afterward, while I get dressed, I tell her that I'm a journalist and that I'm doing a major book about prostitutes.

Wham—a smile!

And that I need her to tell me a little about her life if she wouldn't mind.

'Is that really true? You're a journalist?'

Wham—a smile!

'Yes, well, a journalist student.'

She talks to me. I watch her breasts heave gently as she gets enthusiastic. I dare not believe it. A woman is talking to me, to me. A woman. Smile. She talks. Smile. She keeps talking.

In the evening when my father comes home, I help him take off his coat as usual, then slip around to face him, standing in the light so that I can be sure he sees me.

'Dinner is ready.'

Wham—a smile!

He looks at me in astonishment.

I continue smiling. It's tiring by the end of the day, but I hang in there.

'What did you do? Something stupid, no doubt.'

Then the smile disappears.

But I won't despair.

Over dessert I try again.

Wham—a smile!

He stares at me uncomfortably.

'Come here,' he says.

I sense that my smile is about to win him over. There we go, another victim. I go over to him. Perhaps he wants to kiss me? One time he told me that Popol really liked to kiss him, that he was a very affectionate boy. Perhaps Popol had understood the smiling trick from birth? Or maybe my mother had the time to teach him.

I'm close to my father now, leaning against his

shoulder. His eyelashes are blinking hard. Me, I'm smiling until it hurts.

'We'll have to get you some braces. I never noticed that your teeth protrude.'

That evening I started making it a habit to go and see Monsieur Ibrahim once my father was in bed.

'It's my own fault. If I were more like Popol, my father would love me better.'

'How do you know? Popol left.'

'So?'

'Perhaps he couldn't stand your father.'

'You think so?'

'He left. That proves it, no?'

Monsieur Ibrahim gave me his small change so I could put it into rolls. That calmed me down a little.

'Did you know him? Popol? Monsieur Ibrahim, did you know Popol? What did you think of him, of Popol?'

He hit the till once as if to keep it from talking.

'Momo, I'll tell you one thing. I like you a hundred, a thousand times better than Popol.'

'Really?'

I was quite thrilled but didn't want to show it. I tightened my fists and bared my teeth a little. Must defend your family.

'Careful! I can't let you say bad things about my brother. What did you have against Popol?'

'He was alright Popol, quite all right. But you'll forgive me if I prefer Momo.'

I forgave him.

A week later, Monsieur Ibrahim sent me to see a friend of his, the dentist of the Rue Papillon. He had a lot of influence, Monsieur Ibrahim did, no question about that. And the next day he said to me:

'Momo, smile a little less, it's enough already. No, that was just a joke... My friend assured me that you won't need any braces.'

He leaned over to me with his laughing eyes.

'Just imagine, in the Rue de Paradis, you with scrap metal all over your mouth. There wouldn't be a single one of them who'd still believe that you are sixteen.'

Now he really hit a bull's-eye, Monsieur Ibrahim.

As a result, I asked him for his change so I could calm down.

'How do you know all that, Monsieur Ibrahim?'

'Me, I know nothing. I only know what it says in my Koran.'

I made a few more rolls.

'Momo, there's nothing wrong with going to the professionals. The first few times you should always go to professionals, women who know their job really well. Later on, when you get involved and it gets to be more complicated, when feelings are added, then you can make do with amateurs.'

I felt better.

'Do you go there sometimes, the Rue de Paradis?'

'Paradise is open to everyone.'

'Oh, you're teasing, Monsieur Ibrahim, you're not going to tell me you still go there at your age?'

'Why? Is it reserved for minors only?'

Then I knew I had said something stupid.

'Momo, how about taking a walk with me?'

'Oh really, you walk sometimes, too?'

And again I knew I'd said something stupid.

So I added a huge smile.

'What I mean is that I always see you just sitting on this stool.'

I was really excited, though.

The following day, Monsieur Ibrahim took me to Paris, the Paris that is pretty, the one in the photographs, of the tourists. We walked along the Seine, which isn't really straight.

'Look, Momo, the Seine loves bridges, like a woman who's crazy about bracelets.'

Then we walked through the parks along the Champs-Elysées, between the theatres and the puppet show. Then the Rue du Faubourg-Saint-Honoré, where there were lots of designer stores with brand names like Lanvin, Hermès, Saint Laurent, and Cardin. It felt odd, these huge and empty shops next to Monsieur Ibrahim's grocery store that was no bigger than a bathroom, but where there wasn't an inch that went unused, where every item—vital or not vital—was piled up from floor to ceiling, from shelf to shelf, three rows high and four rows deep.

'It's crazy, Monsieur Ibrahim, how the shop windows of the rich are so poor. There's nothing in it.'

'That's what luxury is, Momo, nothing in the window, nothing in the shop, everything in the price.'

We ended with the secret gardens of the Palais-Royal where Monsieur Ibrahim bought me fresh lemonade and rediscovered his legendary immobility on a barstool, slowly sipping his anise Suze.

'It must be nice to live in Paris.'

'But you are living in Paris, Momo.'

'No, I live in the Rue Bleue.'

I watched him enjoy his anise Suze.

'I thought that Muslims didn't drink alcohol.'

'True, but I'm a Sufi.'

That's when I sensed I was being indiscreet, that Monsieur Ibrahim didn't want to tell me about his disease—after all, that was his right; I stayed quiet until we were back in the Rue Bleue.

That evening I opened my father's dictionary. I must have been really worried about Monsieur

Ibrahim because, really, dictionaries have always disappointed me.

'Sufism: a mystical branch of Islam, dating from the eighth century. Opposed to legalism, it emphasises religion inside the person.'

There I was, once again! Dictionaries clearly explain only those words you already know.

In any event, Sufism was not a disease, which reassured me somewhat. It was a way of thinking—even if there are ways of thinking that are also diseases, as Monsieur Ibrahim often said. After this I went off on a treasure hunt to try and understand all the words in the definition. From this it became clear that Monsieur Ibrahim with his anise Suze believed in God in the Muslim way, but in a manner that bordered on smuggling for it was 'opposed to legalism' and that really gave me a hard time because if legalism was, indeed, the 'strict conformity to the law' as the dictionary people were saying... well, in general terms that meant disturbing things a priori, namely that Monsieur Ibrahim was dishonest, and thus that the people I frequented were not respectable. But at the same time, if respecting the law was being a lawyer, as my father was, having the grey complexion and so much sadness in the house, I'd rather be against legalism and with Monsieur Ibrahim. And the dictionary people added that Sufism had been created by two ancient guys, al-Halladj and al-Ghazali, names that should be living in the attic rooms in the back of the courtyard—in the Rue Bleue, in any case—and they specified that it was an inner religion and there Monsieur Ibrahim surely was discreet.

During dinner, I couldn't help myself and questioned my father who was busy gulping down a lamb stew, Royal Canine style.

'Dad do you believe in God?'

He looked at me. Then, slowly, he said:

'I can see that you are becoming a man.'

I didn't get the connection. For a moment I even wondered if someone had reported to him that I was seeing the girls of the Rue de Paradis. But then he added:

'No, I've never managed to believe in God.'

'Never managed? Why? Does one have to make an effort?'

He looked around the badly-lit flat.

'To believe that all this has any meaning? Yes. You have to make an enormous effort.'

'But Dad, we're Jews. Well, you and I, aren't we?'

'Yes.'

'And being Jewish has nothing to do with God?'

'For me it no longer does. Being Jewish is merely having memories. Bad memories.'

And then his face really looked like that of someone in desperate need of aspirin. Maybe because he had been talking for a change, which was unusual for him, not in his habits. He got up and went straight to bed.

A few days later, he came home looking even paler than usual. I was beginning to feel guilty. I told myself that by making him eat rubbish I had perhaps derailed his health.

I sat down and he motioned to me that he wanted to tell me something.

But it took him a good ten minutes to get around to it.

'I've been fired, Moses. They don't want me any more in the office where I work.'

Frankly, it didn't really surprise me that they didn't feel like working with my father—for the criminals he must have been depressing to be with—but at the same time I had never imagined that a lawyer could cease to be a lawyer.

'I'll have to look for another job. Somewhere else. We'll have to tighten the belt, my son.'

He went off to bed. Obviously, he wasn't interested in knowing what I was thinking.

I went down to see Monsieur Ibrahim, who was smiling and chewing peanuts.

'How do you manage to be happy, Monsieur Ibrahim?'

'I know what it says in my Koran.'

'Maybe I should pinch that from you one day, your Koran, that is. Even if that's not done when you're Jewish.'

'Phew, what does it mean to you, Momo, being Jewish?'

'Well, I don't know. For my father it means being depressed all day. For me... it's just something that keeps me from being anything else.'

Monsieur Ibrahim gave me a peanut.

'Your shoes are in bad shape, Momo. Tomorrow we'll go and buy you some new shoes.'

'Yes, but...'

'A man spends his life in just two places—either in his bed or in his shoes.'

'I have no money, Monsieur Ibrahim.'

'They're a present. It's my gift to you, Momo. You have only one pair of feet and you should take care of them. If shoes hurt you, you must change them. Feet can't be changed!'

The next day, coming home from school, I found a note on the floor of our unlit hallway. I don't know why but at the sight of my father's handwriting, my heart beat madly in all directions:

Moses,

Forgive me, but I am leaving, I don't have it in me to be a father. Popo...

The next part was crossed out. Without any doubt he wanted to say something about Popol. In the style of 'with Popol I would have managed, but not with you,' or maybe 'Popol gave me the strength and energy to be a father, but not you'— in short, some crappy thing he was ashamed to write down.

Well, I definitely got the message, thank you.

Perhaps we will see each other again one day, later on, when you are older. When I am less ashamed and you have forgiven me.

That's it, farewell!

P.S. I left all the money I have on the table. Here's a list of people whom you should inform of my departure. They will take care of you.

Then there was a list of four names I did not recognise.

My decision was made. I would have to pretend.

Admitting that I had been abandoned was out of the question. Twice abandoned—once by my mother when I was born, and again as a teenager by my father. If this became known, there wouldn't be anyone left that would give me a chance. What was so terrible about me? What was so wrong with me that made love impossible? My decision was irrevocable—I would disguise my father's absence. I would make people believe he was there, he ate there, and that he still shared his long and boring evenings with me.

In fact, I didn't wait at all—I went down to the shop.

'Monsieur Ibrahim, my father has indigestion. What should I give him?'

'Fernet Branca, Momo. Here, I have a little bottle right here.'

'Thank you. I'll run back up and have him take it straight away.'

With the money he had left me, I could manage for a month. I learned to imitate his signature to complete the necessary mail and respond to the school. I continued cooking for two and every night I set his place at the table across from me; the only difference was that at the end of the meal I would throw his down the sink.

A few nights a week, just for the neighbours across the street, I'd sit in his armchair, wear his sweater and shoes, put some flowers in my hair, and tried to read a brand-new Koran Monsieur Ibrahim had given me because I had begged him for one.

At school I told myself I didn't have a moment to lose—I had to fall in love. There wasn't much choice there since mine was not a mixed school. All the boys were in love with Myriam, the caretaker's daughter, who despite her thirteen years had very rapidly understood that she was reigning over three hundred starved teenagers. I started courting her with the fervour of a drowning man.

Wham—a smile!

I had to prove to myself that I could be loved. I had to let the whole world know before they discovered that even my parents, the only ones who were obliged to put up with me, had preferred escape.

I told Monsieur Ibrahim of my conquest of Myriam. He listened to me with the little smile of someone who knows how the story ends, but I preferred not to notice.

'And how's your father? I don't see him in the mornings any more.'

'He's got a lot of work. He has to leave very early now with his new job.'

'Oh really? And he isn't furious about your reading of the Koran?'

'I do it secretly, anyway. And besides, I don't understand very much of what's in it.'

'When you want to learn something, you don't take a book. You talk to someone. I don't believe in books.'

'But still, Monsieur Ibrahim, you're always telling me that you know what...'

'Yes, that I know what it says in my Koran. Momo, I feel like seeing the sea. What if we went to Normandy? I'll take you.'

'Would you really?'

'If your father agrees, of course.'

'He'll agree.'

'Are you sure?'

'I'm telling you, he'll agree.'

When we arrived in the lobby of the Grand Hotel in Cabourg, it was all too much for me—I began to cry. I cried for two or maybe three hours, I could barely stop to catch my breath.

Monsieur Ibrahim watched me cry. He waited patiently for me to start speaking. Finally I managed to blurt out:

'It's too beautiful here, Monsieur Ibrahim. It's much too beautiful. It's not for me. I don't deserve this.'

Monsieur Ibrahim smiled.

'Beauty is everywhere, Momo. Wherever you turn your eyes. Now, that comes from my Koran.'

Then we went for a walk along the shore.

'You know, Momo, if a man hasn't had life revealed to him directly by God, he's not going to find it in a book.'

I talked to him about Myriam, all the more so because I was trying to avoid talking about my father. Having admitted me into her circle of suitors, Myriam was now beginning to reject me as an unworthy candidate.

'It doesn't matter,' Monsieur Ibrahim said. 'Your love for her belongs to you. It's yours. Even if she refuses it, she cannot change it. She isn't benefitting from it, that's all. What you give, Momo, is yours forever. What you keep is lost forever!'

'But you, do you have a wife?'

'Yes.'

'And why then aren't you here with her?'

He pointed to the sea.

'This really is an English sea right here, green and grey. These are not the normal colours of water. You'd think they'd taken on an accent.'

'You didn't answer me, Monsieur Ibrahim about your wife. About your wife?'

'Momo, no answer is also an answer.'

Each morning, Monsieur Ibrahim was up first. He'd go to the window, sniff the light, and slowly do his exercise—every morning, his whole life through, morning exercises. He was incredibly flexible and as I opened my eyes I could still see, from my pillow, the tall and carefree young man he must have been, very long ago.

A great surprise to me was discovering in the bathroom one day that Monsieur Ibrahim was circumcised.

'You, too, Monsieur Ibrahim?'

'Muslims just like Jews, Momo. It's about the sacrifice of Abraham: he holds his child out to God, telling him he may take him. That bit of skin that we don't have is the mark of Abraham. At the circumcision, the father must hold his son, the father offers his own pain in memory of Abraham's sacrifice.'

Through Monsieur Ibrahim, I realised that Jews, Muslims, and even Christians had plenty of great men in common before they began to squabble with each other. It didn't concern me, but it did me good.

After our return from Normandy, when I came home to the dark and empty flat, I didn't feel different but I did sense that the world could be different. I told myself that I could open the windows, that the walls could be lighter. I said to myself that nothing forced me to keep this furniture that smelled of the past, not the good old days, no, the worn and rancid days, those that smell like an old dish cloth.

I had no money left. I began to sell the books in lots to the book vendors on the banks of the Seine that Monsieur Ibrahim had shown me during our walks. Every time I sold a book I felt freer.

It was three months now since my father had vanished. I was still pretending, keeping up appearances, still cooking for two, and strangely enough Monsieur Ibrahim asked after my father less and less frequently. My relationship with Myriam crumbled more and more, but it provided me with a very good topic of conversation for the evenings with Monsieur Ibrahim.

Some nights I felt my heart shrink. That was because I was thinking of Popol. Now that my father was no longer there, I would have liked to get to know Popol. I was sure that I would be better able to stand him since he was no longer being thrown in my face as the antithesis to my worthlessness. I often went to bed thinking that somewhere in the world there was a good-looking and perfect brother who was unknown to me and that maybe I would meet him one day.

One morning the police knocked on the door. They were shouting like they do in the films:

'Open up! Police!'

I said to myself: 'OK, that's it, it's all over. I've been lying too much. They're coming to arrest me.'

I put on a robe and unlocked all the bolts. They looked a lot less mean than I'd imagined, they even asked me politely if they could come in. True, I myself, too, preferred getting dressed before leaving for prison.

In the living room, the inspector took my hand and said very gently:

'Young man, we have some bad news for you. Your father is dead.'

I didn't know right away what astonished me more, my father's death or the formal way the policeman was addressing me. In any case, I collapsed into the armchair.

'He threw himself under a train near Marseilles.'

That was very strange, as well—why go all the way to Marseilles! There are trains everywhere. There are just as many, if not more, in Paris itself. I really would never understand my father.

'There is every indication that your father was desperate and ended his life of his own free will.'

A father that commits suicide, now that was something that wasn't going to make me feel any better. Finally, I wondered if I wouldn't rather have a father who deserts me; at least I could assume that he was being eaten up by remorse.

The officers seemed to understand my silence. They were looking at the empty library, the dreary flat, and must have been thinking how, thankfully, they'd be out of here in just a few more minutes.

'Who should we notify, my boy?'

That's when I had an appropriate reaction at last. I got up and went to look for the list with the four names he had left me. The inspector put it in his pocket.

'We'll give this information to the Social Services.'

Then he came over to me with his hangdog eyes and I could tell he had something hideous for me.

'Now, I have to ask you something delicate: you will have to identify the body.'

That played like an alarm signal. I began to shriek as if someone had pressed the button. The officers were churning around me looking to turn it off. Only, no luck, because the off-button was me and I couldn't stop myself any more.

Monsieur Ibrahim was fantastic. When he heard my screams he came upstairs and instantly grasped the situation. He said he would go to Marseilles himself and identify the body. At first, the police were suspicious because he really looked like an Arab, but I began to shriek again and then they accepted Monsieur Ibrahim's suggestion.

After the burial, I asked Monsieur Ibrahim:

'How long have you known about my father, Monsieur Ibrahim?'

'Since Cabourg. But you know, Momo, you shouldn't hold it against your father.'

'Really? How so? A father who ruins my life, abandons me, and then commits suicide. That's a hell of a lot of trust to give someone to live by. And then after all that, I'm not supposed to hold it against him?'

'Your father had no model to follow. He lost his parents when he was very young because they'd been taken away by the Nazis and died in the camps. Your father never got over having escaped all that. Maybe he felt guilty about being alive. It's not for nothing that he ended up under a train.'

'Oh really, why?'

'His parents had been taken away by a train to go to their death. Perhaps, he had been looking for his train all along... If he didn't have the strength to live it was not because of you, Momo, but because of everything that happened before you.'

Then Monsieur Ibrahim stuffed a few notes into my pocket.

'Here, go to the Rue de Paradis. The girls have been wondering where you're at with that book about them.'

I began to change everything in the flat in the Rue Bleue. Monsieur Ibrahim gave me cans of paint and brushes. He also gave me advice on how to make the social worker crazy and play for time.

One afternoon when I'd opened all the windows wide to let the smell of the acrylic paint out, a woman entered the flat. I don't know why, but I knew right away who she was from her embarrassment, her hesitation, and the way she didn't dare walk between the ladders and was avoiding the spots on the floor.

I pretended to be deeply immersed in the work.

She finally cleared her throat softly.

I acted surprised:

'You are looking for?'

'I'm looking for Moses,' said my mother.

It was odd how she had a hard time pronouncing my name as if she couldn't get it out of her mouth.

I decided to wind her up a bit.

'And who are you?'

'I'm his mother.'

Poor woman, I felt pity for her. She was in such a

state. She must have really forced herself to get to this point.

She looked at me intently, trying to scan my features. She is scared, very scared.

'And you are you?'

'Me?'

I felt like having fun. It's incredible how people can get themselves in such a state, especially after thirteen years.

'Me, they call me Momo.'

Her face shatters.

Laughing, I add:

'It's a diminutive for Mohammed.'

She becomes even paler than the whitewash I was painting on the walls.

'Oh really? You're not Moses?'

'Oh no, you shouldn't confuse the two, Madame. Me, I'm Mohammed.'

She swallows. She's not really unhappy about it when all is said and done.

'But isn't there a boy here whose name is Moses?'

I feel like answering: 'I don't know, you're his

mother, you ought to know.' But at the last moment I hold it in because the poor woman doesn't look very steady on her legs. Instead, I make up a pretty and more comfortable little lie.

'Moses left, Madame. He'd had enough of all of this. He didn't have any good memories.'

'Oh really?'

I'm wondering if she believes me. She doesn't seem convinced. Maybe she isn't so stupid after all.

'And when will he be back?'

'I don't know. When he left he said he went to find his brother.'

'His brother?'

'Yes, Moses has a brother.'

'Oh really?'

She looks utterly bewildered.

'Yes, his brother Popol.'

'Popol?'

'Yes, Madame. Popol, his older brother.'

I'm wondering if perhaps she is taking me for an idiot. Or else she really believes I'm Mohammed.

'But I never had a child before Moses. I never had any Popol.'

Now I'm beginning to feel bad.

She notices it, she is shaking so much that she has to sit down in an armchair and I do the same.

We look at each other in silence, our noses stuffed with the sharp smell of acrylic. She studies me, and there's not a blink of my eyes that escapes her.

'Tell me, Momo...'

'Mohammed.'

'Tell me, Mohammed, will you be seeing Moses again?'

'Possibly.'

I say it in a detached tone, I can't get over the detachment in my voice. She scrutinises me, looks deep into my eyes. She can pick at me as much as she wants, she won't get anything out of me, I'm very sure of myself.

'If you should see Moses again one day, tell him I was very young when I married his father, and that I married him only to get away from my parents. I never loved Moses' father. But I was ready to love Moses. Only, I met another man. Your father...'

'Excuse me?'

'I mean his father, Moses' father, said to me: 'Go then, but leave Moses with me, or else…' So I left. I preferred to start my life over again, a life where there would be some happiness.'

'It's better that way, that's for sure.'

She lowers her eyes.

She comes over to me. I sense she would like to kiss me. I act as if I don't understand. In an imploring voice she asks me:

'You will tell Moses, won't you?'

'Perhaps.'

The same evening, I went back to Monsieur Ibrahim and asked him laughingly:

'So when are you going to adopt me, Monsieur Ibrahim?'

And he answered, laughing also:

'Well, tomorrow if you want, my little Momo.'

We had to fight for it. The official world, the one with its stamps, authorisations, and its civil servants who become aggressive when you wake them up. Nobody wanted to have anything to do with us. But Monsieur Ibrahim was not to be discouraged.

'We already have the no in our pocket, Momo. We have to acquire the yes.'

My mother, with the help of the social worker, ended up by going along with Monsieur Ibrahim's efforts.

'And what about your wife, Monsieur Ibrahim?' I asked. 'Has she agreed?'

'My wife went back to the old country a long time ago. I do what I want. But if you would like to, we can go and see her this summer.'

The day we obtained it, the document, the famous document that declared I was henceforth the son of the man I had chosen, Monsieur Ibrahim decided that we should buy a car to celebrate.

'We'll take trips, Momo. And this summer, we'll go to the Golden Crescent together. I will show you the sea, the one and only sea, the sea where I come from.'

'Couldn't we go there by flying carpet maybe?'

'Take some brochures and choose a car.'

'Yes, Dad.'

It's weird how you can have very different feelings using the same words. When I said 'Dad' to him my heart was smiling, I swelled with pride, and the future was shining.

We went to the garage owner.

'I want to buy this model here. It's the one my son chose.'

As for Monsieur Ibrahim, he was worse than I when it came to the question of vocabulary. He was adding 'my son' to every sentence, as if he had just invented fatherhood.

The salesman started to go on about the features of the car.

'Don't bother trying to sell it to me. I already told you I want to buy it.'

'Do you have a driving licence, sir?'

'Of course.'

And Monsieur Ibrahim took a document out of his Moroccan leather wallet that must have, at the very least, dated from the Egyptian era. The salesman examined the papyrus with horror, first of all because most of the letters were washed out, and second because it was in a language he didn't know.

'Is this thing a driving licence?'

'Isn't that obvious?'

'Fine. Well then, we suggest that you pay in several monthly instalments. For instance, over a period of three years, you should...'

'When I tell you that I want to purchase a car, it's because I can afford to do so. I'm paying in cash.'

Monsieur Ibrahim was very annoyed. The salesman was really committing one blunder after another.

'Well then, write us a cheque...'

'That's enough! I'm telling you I'm paying cash. With money. Real money.'

And he put wads of bank notes on the table, lovely wads of old notes neatly packed in plastic bags.

The salesman almost choked.

'But... but... nobody pays in cash... that... that's not possible...'

'Well, what's the problem? Are you saying this is not money then? I certainly accepted them in my till, so why shouldn't you? Momo, is this a serious outfit we've come to?'

'Fine. We'll do it your way. We shall make the car available to you in two weeks.'

'Two weeks? That's impossible—I'll be dead by then!'

Two days later, they delivered the car to the shop. He's really something, Monsieur Ibrahim.

When he got into the car, Monsieur Ibrahim began to touch the various controls carefully with his long and slender fingers; then he wiped his forehead, turning green.

'I don't know anymore, Momo.'

'But didn't you learn?'

'Yes, a long time ago, from my friend Abdullah. But...'

'But?'

'But cars were different then.'

He really was having a hard time knowing what to say or do.

'Tell me, Monsieur Ibrahim, the kind of cars you

learned in, were they horse-drawn?'

'No, my little Momo. Donkeys. Drawn by donkeys.'

'And that driving licence the other day, what was that?'

'Hmm... an old letter from my friend Abdullah, telling me how the harvest had been.'

'Well, we're up shit creek!'

'You said it, Momo.'

'And there's nothing in your Koran that would offer a solution, as always?'

'What are you thinking, Momo, that the Koran is a driver's manual? It's useful for things of the spirit, not for scrap iron. And besides, in the Koran they travel by camel!'

'Don't get all worked up, Monsieur Ibrahim.'

In the end, Monsieur Ibrahim decided that we should take driving lessons together. Since I wasn't old enough yet, he was the one who officially was learning while I sat in the back seat without missing one iota of the teacher's instructions. As soon as the lesson was over, we'd take our car and I would be in the driver's seat. We'd drive around Paris by night to avoid the traffic.

I was getting better and better at it.

At last summer arrived and we took to the road.

Thousands of miles. We crossed all of Europe by the southern route. Windows open. We were going to the Middle East. It was an unbelievable discovery to see how interesting the universe became as soon as you travelled with Monsieur Ibrahim. Since I was clutching the steering wheel and concentrating on the road, he would describe the landscape, sky, clouds, villages, and people to me. Monsieur Ibrahim's chatter, his voice as thin as cigarette paper, the flavour of his accent, the images, exclamations, and surprises, followed by the most diabolic tricks, all that is what the road from Paris to Istanbul means to me. I did not see Europe, I heard it.

'Oh, now, Momo, we've reached the affluent— look there are dustbins.'

'Dustbins, so what?'

'When you want to know whether you're in a rich

or poor area, you should look at the dustbins. If you see dustbins but no rubbish, it's wealthy. If you see rubbish next to the dustbins, then it's neither rich nor poor—it's a tourist district. If you see rubbish without any dustbins, then it's poor. And if the people live in the rubbish, then it's very, very poor, indeed. Here we are in a rich area.'

'Well, sure, it's Switzerland.'

'Oh no, Momo, not the motorway. All the motorway is good for is to tell you to keep moving. There's nothing to see. That's for idiots that want to go as fast as possible from one point to another. We're not doing geometry here, we're travelling. Find me some pretty little roads that show us all there is to see.'

'You can tell it's not you who is doing the driving, Monsieur Ibrahim.'

'Listen, Momo, if you don't want to see anything, then you take a plane like everyone else.'

'Is it poor here, Monsieur Ibrahim?'

'Yes, it's Albania.'

'And there?'

'Stop the car. You smell this? It smells of happiness, this is Greece. People don't move, they take the time to watch us pass by, they breathe. You see, Momo, all my life I'll have worked hard, but I'll have worked slowly, taking my time. I didn't just want to ring up numbers or watch the customers parade in and out, no. Slowness, that the secret of happiness. What do you want to do later on?'

'Don't know, Monsieur Ibrahim. Yes, I do. I'll work in import-export.'

Now I'd scored a point. I had found the magic word. Monsieur Ibrahim couldn't stop talking about import-export. It was a serious word and yet adventurous, a word that evoked journeys, ships, packages, big turnovers, a word as heavy as the syllables that it rolled over—import-export!

'Let me introduce my son to you, Momo, who will be in import-export one day.'

We had plenty of games. He had me go into religious places blindfolded so that I would guess the religion by its scent.

'It smells like candles here. It's Catholic.'

'Yes, it is Saint Anthony.'

'This is incense. It's Orthodox.'

'You're right, it's Saint Sophia.'

'And here it smells like feet. It's Muslim. But I mean, really, it stinks too much...'

'What! It's the Blue Mosque! A place that smells of human bodies isn't good enough for you?' Is that because your feet never smell? A place of prayer that smells of men, is made for men, with men inside, that's disgusting to you? You really have some very Parisian ideas, don't you! I find the smell of socks comforting. I remind myself that I am no better than my neighbour. I smell myself, I smell us, and so I already feel better!'

From Istanbul on, Monsieur Ibrahim talked less. He was emotionally touched.

'Soon we will reach the sea where I am from.'

Each day he wanted us to drive more slowly. He wanted to savour it all. He was afraid, also.

'Where is that sea that you come from, Monsieur Ibrahim? Show me on the map.'

'Oh, don't bother me with your maps, Momo.

We're not in school now!'

We stopped in a mountain village.

'I'm happy, Momo. You're here and I know what it says in my Koran. Now I want to take you out dancing.'

'Dancing, Monsieur Ibrahim?'

'We have to. Absolutely. 'A man's heart is like a bird locked inside the cage of the body.' When you dance, the heart sings like a bird aspiring to a fusion with God. Come, lets go to the tekké.'

'To the what?'

'Strange club!' I said as we came through the door.

'A tekké is not a club. It's a monastery. Momo, take off your shoes and put them down.'

And that is where I saw men whirl for the first time. The dervishes wore large pale robes, heavy and soft. A drum reverberated. And the monks turned into spinning tops.

'You see, Momo! They are whirling around, they're turning around their own heart, the place where God is present. It's like a prayer.'

'You call that a prayer?'

'Of course, Momo. They lose every earthly reference point, the heaviness we call equilibrium, and they become torches that are consumed in a huge fire. Try it, Momo, just try it. Follow me.'

And Monsieur Ibrahim and I began to whirl.

With the first few rounds, I said to myself:

I am happy with Monsieur Ibrahim. Then I thought: I'm no longer angry with my father for having left. In the end, I even thought: After all, my mother didn't really have any choice when she...

'So, Momo, did you feel good things?'

'Yeah, it was incredible. My hate was draining away. If the drums hadn't stopped I might have tried to justify my mother's case. It was really nice to pray, Monsieur Ibrahim, even though I would have liked praying better with my trainers on. The heavier a body becomes, the lighter the spirit.'

After that day, we stopped often to dance in tekkés Monsieur Ibrahim was familiar with. Sometimes he didn't whirl and was just happy to have some tea with his eyes half-closed, but I would whirl like a madman.

No, actually I was whirling to become a little less mad.

In the evening in the village squares, I tried to talk to the girls a bit. I did my utmost but it wasn't going terribly well, while Monsieur Ibrahim did nothing but drink his anise Suze and smile with that sweet and calm look of his and, well within an hour he always had lots of people around him.

'You move too much, Momo. If you want to have friends, you shouldn't budge.'

'Monsieur Ibrahim, do you think I'm good-looking?'

'You're very handsome, Momo.'

'No, that's not what I mean. Do you think that I'll be good-looking enough to attract any girls... without having to pay?'

'In a few years they will be paying for you!'

'Still... for now... it's all rather quiet.'

'Obviously, Momo, have you noticed how you're going about it? You stare at them as if wanting to say: 'See how handsome I am.' Well, of course they laugh. You should look at them as if you want to say: 'I've never seen anyone more beautiful than you.' For an ordinary man, I mean like you and me—not Alain Delon or Marlon Brando—your looks are what you find in the woman.'

We watched the sun slide between the mountains and the sky turn violet. Dad stared at the evening star.

'A ladder has been placed before us by which to escape, Momo. First man was mineral, then vegetable, then animal—then he became a man, endowed with knowledge, reason, and faith. Can you imagine the distance you've already covered, from dust till today? And later, when you have gone beyond your human condition, you will become an angel. You'll be done with earth. When you dance, you have a foretaste of that.'

'Maybe. I, for one, don't remember anything. Do you remember having been a plant, Monsieur Ibrahim?'

'Well, what do you think I'm doing when I sit there without moving for hours on my stool in the shop?'

Then the famous day arrived when Monsieur

Ibrahim announced we were going to the sea of his birth to meet his friend Abdullah. He was completely nonplussed, like a young man. He wanted to go there by himself first to find the place, and asked me to wait for him under an olive tree.

It was siesta time. I fell asleep against the tree.

When I woke up, the day was gone. I waited for Monsieur Ibrahim until midnight.

I walked to the next village. When I reached the square, people rushed over to me. I didn't understand their language, but they were speaking very excitedly and seemed to know me very well. They brought me to a large house. First I went through a long room where several women were crouching and moaning. Then they brought me to Monsieur Ibrahim.

He was lying down, covered with wounds, bruises, and blood. The car had run into a wall.

He looked terribly weak.

I threw myself upon him. He opened his eyes and smiled.

'Momo, this is where the journey ends.'

'Oh no, we haven't arrived there yet, at the sea of your birth.'

'Yes, I'm there. Every branch of the river comes out into the same sea. The one and only sea.'

Then, in spite of myself, I began to cry.

'Momo, I'm not happy.'

'I'm afraid for you, Monsieur Ibrahim.'

'Me, I'm not afraid, Momo. I know what it says in my Koran.'

That was a sentence he shouldn't have spoken. It brought back too many good memories, and so I began to sob even more.

'Momo, you are crying for yourself, not for me. I have lived a good life. I have lived to be old. I have had a wife who died a very long time ago but whom I still love just as much. I had my friend Abdullah, and you will give him my warmest greetings. My little shop did well. The Rue Bleue is a nice street even if it isn't blue. And then there was you.'

Just to please him, I swallowed the rest of my tears and made an effort and wham—a smile!

He was happy. It seemed he was in less pain.

Wham—a smile!

He gently closed his eyes.

'Monsieur Ibrahim!'

'Shh... don't worry. I'm not dying, Momo, I'm going to join infinity.'

There it is.

I stayed for a while. I spoke about Dad a lot with his friend Addullah. We did a lot of whirling, too.

Monsieur Abdullah was like Monsieur Ibrahim, but a parchment version of Monsieur Ibrahim, full of unusual words and poems that he knew by heart, a Monsieur Ibrahim who had spent more time reading than making his till ring. He called the hours we spent whirling in the tekké the dance of alchemy, the dance that changes copper into gold.

He often quoted Rumi and would say:

Gold does not need the philosopher's stone
but copper does.
Improve yourself.
Let die what is alive: that is your body.
Revive what is dead: that is your heart.

Hide what is present: that is the world down here.
Let come what is absent: that is the future.
Annihilate what exists: that is passion.
Produce what does not exist: that is intention.

Thus, even today, when things are going badly, I whirl.

I turn one hand toward the sky and I whirl. I turn one hand toward the ground and I whirl. The sky turns above me. The earth turns below me. I am no longer my self but one of those atoms that turns around the void that is everything.

As Monsieur Ibrahim used to say:

'Your intelligence is in your ankles and your ankles have a very profound way of thinking.'

I hitchhiked back. I put myself into 'the hands of God' as Monsieur Ibrahim used to say when he was talking about the homeless. I begged and I slept under the open sky and that, too, was quite a beautiful gift. I didn't want to spend the money Monsieur Abdullah had slipped into my pocket when he kissed me just before I left him.

Back in Paris, I discovered that Monsieur Ibrahim had anticipated everything. He had set me free. I inherited his money, his shop, and his Koran.

The lawyer gave me the grey envelope and I tenderly took out the old book. At last I was going to find out what it said in his Koran.

In his Koran were two dried flowers and a letter from his friend Abdullah.

Now I am Momo and everybody in the street knows me. In the end I didn't go into import-export, which I had only said to make a bit of an impression on Monsieur Ibrahim.

From time to time my mother comes to see me. She calls me Mohammed so that I won't get angry and she asks me for news from Moses, which I give her.

Recently, I told her that Moses had found his brother Popol again and they had left on a trip together and that, as far as I could tell, we wouldn't see them any time soon. Perhaps it wasn't worth discussing any more. She thought for a long time— she is always on her guard with me—then she murmured gently:

'After all, maybe it's better that way. There are some forms of childhood you should leave behind, there are some that need healing.'

I told her psychology wasn't my field; the shop was who I was.

'I'd like to invite you for dinner one evening. Mohammed. My husband would like to meet you, too.'

'What does he do?'

'He teaches English.'

'And you?'

'I teach Spanish.'

'And what language do we speak at dinner? No, I was only joking. I'd like that.'

She flushed pink with delight that I had accepted. No, really it's true, it was a pleasure to watch—you would have though I had just installed running water for her.

'Really? You mean it? You'll come?'

'Yeah, yeah.'

What is certain is that it is a little strange to have two teachers from the state education system receive Mohammed, the grocer, but then again, why not? I'm not racist.

There it is… it's become a habit. I go to their house every Monday with my wife and children. They're so affectionate, my kids, they call her—the Spanish teacher— Grandma and you should see how that thrills her! Sometimes she is so elated that she gingerly asks me if it doesn't bother me. I tell her no, that I have a sense of humour.

So, now I am Momo, the one who has the shop in the Rue Bleue, the Rue Bleue that isn't blue.

In everybody's eyes I am the local Arab.

In the grocery business, being Arab means being open at night and on Sundays.

the End

Eric-Emmanuel Schmitt's

Trilogy of the Unseen

comprises:

Monsieur Ibrahim and the Flowers of the Koran

Oscar and the Pink Lady

Milarepa

Other acorn titles include:

the girl from chimel

Tales from a Mayan village.
by Nobel Prize Winner
Rigoberta Menchú

£6.99 ISBN 0-9534205-7-4

snow
by Maxence Fermine
'Yuko Akita had two passions.
Haiku.
And snow.'

£5.99 ISBN 0-953405-3-1

brown
by Franck Pavloff
The new regime wanted everything to be brown.
Anything else would disappear. First the cats, then the
dogs, then the people.
600,000 copies sold

£2.99 ISBN 0-9544959-1-8

Titles are available direct from
acorn book company
PO Box 191, Tadworth
Surrey KT20 5YQ

POST FREE IN THE UK

Cheques payable to acorn book company.

acorn book company

is an independent
publisher of small, high quality editions.

We also operate a mail order web-site.

For more information
please visit us at:
www.acornbook.co.uk